UMNEY'S LAST CASE

STEPHEN KING

UMNEY'S LAST CASE

penguin books

PENGUIN BOOKS
Published by the Penguin Group
Penguin Books USA Inc., 375 Hudson Street,
New York, New York 10014, U.S.A.
Penguin Books Ltd, 27 Wrights Lane,
London W8 5TZ, England
Penguin Books Australia Ltd, Ringwood,
Victoria, Australia
Penguin Books Canada Ltd, 10 Alcorn Avenue,
Toronto, Ontario, Canada M4V 3B2
Penguin Books (N.Z.) Ltd, 182–190 Wairau Road,
Auckland 10, New Zealand

Penguin Books Ltd, Registered Offices:
Harmondsworth, Middlesex, England

Published in Penguin Books 1995

"Umney's Last Case" was first published in
Mr. King's *Nightmares and Dreamscapes*, Viking Penguin, 1993.

ISBN 0 14 60.0074 9

Printed in the United States of America

The rains are over. The hills are still green and in the valley across the Hollywood hills you can see snow on the high mountains. The fur stores are advertising their annual sales. The call houses that specialize in sixteen-year-old virgins are doing a land-office business. And in Beverly Hills the jacaranda trees are beginning to bloom.

—*Raymond Chandler,*
The Little Sister

I. The News from Peoria.

It was one of those spring mornings so L.A.-perfect you keep expecting to see that little trademark symbol—®—stamped on it somewhere. The exhaust of the vehicles passing on Sunset smelled faintly of oleander, the oleander was lightly perfumed with exhaust, and the sky overhead was as clear as a hardshell Baptist's conscience. Peoria Smith, the blind paperboy, was standing in his accustomed place on the corner of Sunset and Laurel, and if that didn't mean God was in His heaven and all was jake with the world, I didn't know what did.

Yet since I'd swung my feet out of bed that morning at the unaccustomed hour of 7:30 A.M., things had felt a little off-kilter, somehow; a tad woozy around the edges. It was only as I was shaving—or at least showing those pesky bristles the razor in an effort to scare them into submission—that I realized part of the reason why. Although I'd been up reading until at least two, I hadn't heard the Demmicks roll in, squiffed to the earlobes and trading those snappy one-liners that apparently form the basis of their marriage.

Nor had I heard Buster, and that was maybe even odder. Buster, the Demmicks' Welsh Corgi, has a high-pitched bark that goes through your head like slivers of glass, and he uses it as much as he can. Also, he's the jealous type. He lets loose with one of his shrill barking squalls every time George and Gloria clinch, and when they aren't zinging each other like a couple of vaudeville comedians, George and Gloria usually *are* clinching. I've gone to sleep on more than one occasion listening to them giggle while that mutt prances around their feet going *yarkyarkyark* and wondering how difficult it would be to strangle a muscular, medium-sized dog with a length of pianowire. Last night, however, the Demmicks' apartment had been as quiet as the grave. It was passing strange, but a long way from earth-shattering; the Demmicks weren't exactly your perfect life-on-a-timetable couple at the best of times.

Peoria Smith was all right, though—chipper as a chipmunk, just as always, and he'd recognized me by my walk even though it was at least an hour before my usual time. He was wearing a baggy CalTech sweatshirt that came down to his thighs and a pair of corduroy knickers that showed off his scabby knees. His hated white cane leaned casually against the side of the card-table he did business on.

"Say, Mr. Umney! Howza kid?"

Peoria's dark glasses glinted in the morning sunlight, and as he turned toward the sound of my step with my copy of the *L.A. Times* held up in front of him, I had a momentary unsettling thought: it was as if someone had drilled two big black holes into his face. I shivered the thought off my back, thinking that maybe the time had come to cut out the before-bedtime shot of rye. Either that or double the dose.

Hitler was on the front of the *Times*, as he so often was these days. This time it was something about Austria. I thought, and not for the first time, how at home that pale face and limp forelock would have looked on a post-office bulletin board.

"The kid is just about okay, Peoria," I said. "In fact, the kid is as fine as fresh paint on an outhouse wall."

I dropped a dime into the Corona box resting atop Peoria's stack of newspapers. The *Times* is a three-center, and overpriced at that, but I've been dropping that same chip into Peoria's change-box since time out of mind. He's a good kid, and making good grades in school—I took it on myself to check that last year, after he'd helped me out on the Weld case. If Peoria hadn't shown up on

Harris Brunner's houseboat when he did, I'd still be trying to swim with my feet cemented into a kerosene drum, somewhere off Malibu. To say I owe him a lot is an understatement.

In the course of that particular investigation (Peoria Smith, not Harris Brunner and Mavis Weld), I even found out the kid's real name, although wild horses wouldn't have dragged it out of me. Peoria's father took a permanent coffee-break out a ninth-floor office window on Black Friday, his mother's the only white frail working in that goofy Chinese laundry down on La Punta, and the kid's blind. With all that, does the world need to know they hung Francis on him when he was too young to fight back? The defense rests.

If anything really juicy happened the night before, you almost always find it on the front page of the *Times*, left side, just below the fold. I turned the newspaper over and saw that a bandleader of the Cuban persuasion had suffered a heart attack while dancing with his female vocalist at The Carousel in Burbank. He died an hour later at L.A. General. I had some sympathy for the maestro's widow, but none for the man himself. My opinion is that people who go dancing in Burbank deserve what they get.

I opened to the sports section to see how Brooklyn had done in their doubleheader with the Cards the day before.

4

"How about you, Peoria? Everyone holding their own in your castle? Moats and battlements all in good repair?"

"I'll say, Mr. Umney! Oh, boy!"

Something in his voice caught my attention, and I lowered the paper to take a closer look at him. When I did, I saw what a gilt-edged shamus like me should have seen right away: the kid was all but busting with happiness.

"You look like somebody just gave you six tickets to the first game of the World Series," I said. "What's the buzz, Peoria?"

"My mom hit the lottery down in Tijuana!" he said. "Forty thousand bucks! We're rich, brother! *Rich!*"

I gave him a grin he couldn't see and ruffled his hair. It popped his cowlick up, but what the hell. "Whoa, hold the phone. How old are you, Peoria?"

"Twelve in May. *You* know that, Mr. Umney, you gave me a polo-shirt. But I don't see what this has to do with—"

"Twelve's old enough to know that sometimes people get what they *want* to happen mixed up with what actually *does* happen. That's all I meant."

"If you're talkin about daydreams, you're right—I *do* know all about em," Peoria said, running his hands over the back of his head in an effort to make his cowlick lie down again, "but this ain't no daydream, Mr. Umney. It's

5

real! My Uncle Fred went down and picked up the cash yest'y afternoon. He brought it back in the saddlebag of his Vinnie! I smelled it! Hell, I *rolled* in it! It was spread all over my mom's bed! Richest feeling I ever had, let me tell you—forty-froggin-thousand smackers!"

"Twelve may be old enough to know the difference between daydreams and what's real, but it's not old enough for that kind of talk," I said. It sounded good—I'm sure the Legion of Decency would have approved two thousand per cent—but my mouth was running on automatic pilot, and I barely heard what was coming out of it. I was too busy trying to get my brain wrapped around what he'd just told me. Of one thing I was absolutely positive: he'd made a mistake. He *must* have made a mistake, because if it was true, then Peoria wouldn't be standing here anymore when I came by on my way to my office in the Fulwider Building. And that just couldn't be.

I found my mind returning to the Demmicks, who for the first time in recorded history hadn't played any of their big-band records at full volume before retiring, and to Buster, who for the first time in recorded history hadn't greeted the sound of George's latchkey turning in the lock with a fusillade of barks. The thought that something was off-kilter returned, and it was stronger this time.

Meanwhile, Peoria was looking at me with an expression I'd never expected to see on his honest, open face: sulky irritation mixed with exasperated humor. It was the way a kid looks at a windbag uncle who's told all his stories, even the boring ones, three or four times.

"Ain't you picking up on this newsflash, Mr. Umney? We're *rich!* My mom ain't going to have to press shirts for that damned old Lee Ho anymore, and I ain't going to have to sell papers on the corner anymore, shiverin when it rains in the winter and havin to suck up to those nutty old bags who work down at Bilder's. I can quit actin like I died and went to heaven every time some blowhard leaves me a nickel tip."

I started a little at that, but what the hell—I wasn't a nickel man. I left Peoria seven cents, day in and day out. Unless I was too broke to afford it, of course, but in my business an occasional stony stretch comes with the territory.

"Maybe we ought to go up to Blondie's and have a cup of java," I said. "Talk this thing over."

"Can't. It's closed."

"Blondie's? The hell you say!"

But Peoria couldn't be bothered with such mundane stuff as the coffee shop in the street. "You ain't heard the best, Mr. Umney! My Uncle Fred knows a doctor up in

7

Frisco—a specialist—who thinks he can do something about my eyes." He turned his face up to mine. Below the cheaters and his too-thin nose, his lips were trembling. "He says it might not be the optic nerves after all, and if it's not, there's an operation . . . I don't understand all the technical stuff, but I could see again, Mr. Umney!" He reached out for me blindly . . . well, of course he did. How else *could* he reach out? *"I could see again!"*

He clutched at me, and I gripped his hands and squeezed them briefly before pushing them gently away. There was ink on his fingers, and I'd been feeling so good when I got up that I'd put on my new chalk worsted. Hot for summer, of course, but the whole city is air-conditioned these days, and besides, I was feeling naturally cool.

I didn't feel so cool now. Peoria was looking up at me, his thin and somehow perfect newsboy's face troubled. A little breeze—scented with oleander and exhaust—ruffled his cowlick, and I realized that I could see it because he wasn't wearing his tweed cap. He looked somehow naked without it, and why not? *Every* newsboy should wear a tweed cap, just like every shoeshine boy should wear a beanie cocked way back on his head.

"What's the matter, Mr. Umney? I thought you'd be happy. Jeepers, I didn't *have* to come out here to this lousy corner today, you know, but I did—I even got here early, because I kinda had an idea *you'd* get here early. I thought you'd be happy, my mom hittin the lottery and me gettin a chance at an operation, but you ain't." Now his voice trembled with resentment. "You ain't!"

"Yes I am," I said, and I *wanted* to be happy—part of me did, anyway—but the bitch of it was that he was mostly right. Because it meant things would change, you see, and things weren't *supposed* to change. Peoria Smith was supposed to be right here, year in and year out, with that perfect cap of his tilted back on hot days and pulled down low on rainy ones, so that the raindrops dripped off the bill. He was always supposed to be smiling, was never supposed to say "hell" or "frogging," and most of all, he was supposed to be *blind*.

"You *ain't!*" he said, and then, shockingly, he pushed his card-table over. It fell into the street, papers flapping everywhere. His white cane rolled into the gutter. Peoria heard it go and bent down to get it. I could see tears coming out from beneath his dark glasses and go rolling down his pale, thin cheeks. He started groping for the cane, but it had fallen near me and he was going the wrong way. I felt a sudden strong urge to haul off and kick him in his blind newsboy's ass.

Instead, I bent over, got his stick, and tapped him lightly on the hip with it.

Peoria turned, quick as a snake, and snatched it. Out of the corner of my eye I could see pictures of Hitler and the recently deceased Cuban bandleader flapping all over Sunset Boulevard—a bus bound for Van Ness snored through a little drift of them, leaving a bitter tang of diesel fumes behind. I hated the way those newspapers looked, fluttering here and there. They looked messy. Worse, they looked *wrong*. Utterly and completely *wrong*. I fought another urge, as strong as the first one, to grab Peoria and shake him. To tell him he was going to spend the morning picking up those newspapers, and I wasn't going to let him go home until he'd gotten every last one.

It occurred to me that less than ten minutes ago, I'd been thinking that this was the perfect L.A. morning—so perfect it deserved a trademark symbol. And it *had* been, dammit. So where had things gone wrong? And how had it happened so fast?

No answers came, only an irrational but powerful voice from inside, telling me that the kid's mother *couldn't* have won the lottery, that the kid *couldn't* stop selling newspapers, and that, most of all, the kid couldn't see. Peoria Smith was supposed to be blind for the rest of his life.

Well, it's got to be something experimental, I thought. *Even if the doctor up in Frisco isn't a quack, and he probably is, the operation's bound to fail.*

And, bizarre as it sounds, the thought calmed me down.

"Listen," I said, "we got off on the wrong foot this morning, that's all. Let me make it up to you. We'll go down to Blondie's and I'll buy you breakfast. What do you say, Peoria? You can dig into a plate of bacon and eggs and tell me all ab—"

"Fuck you!" he shouted, shocking me all the way down to my shoes. "Fuck you and the horse you rode in on, you cheap gumshoe! You think blind people can't tell when people like you are lying through their teeth? Fuck you! And keep your hands off me from now on! I think you're a faggot!"

That did it—no one calls me a faggot and gets away with it, not even a blind newsboy. I forgot all about how Peoria had saved my life during that Mavis Weld business; I reached for his cane, meaning to take it away from him and whack him across the keister with it a few times. Teach him some manners.

Before I could get it, though, he hauled off and slammed the cane's tip into my lower belly—and I *do* mean lower. I doubled up in agony, but even while I was trying to keep from howling with pain, I was counting my blessings; two inches lower still and I could have quit peeping for a living and gotten a job singing soprano in the Palace of the Doges.

I made a quick, reflexive grab for him anyway, and he brought the cane down on the back of my neck. Hard. It didn't break, but I heard it crack. I figured I could finish the job when I caught him and ran it into his right ear. I'd show him who was a faggot.

He backed away from me as if he'd caught my brainwave, and threw the cane into the street.

"Peoria," I managed. Maybe it still wasn't too late to catch sanity by the shirttail. "Peoria, what the hell's wrong with—"

"*And don't call me that!*" he screamed. "*My name's Francis! Frank! You're the one who started calling me Peoria! You started it and now everyone calls me that and I hate it!*"

My watering eyes doubled him as he turned and fled across the street, heedless of traffic (of which there was currently none, luckily for him), hands held out in front of him. I thought he would trip over the far curb—was looking forward to it, in fact—but I guess blind people must keep a pretty good set of topographical survey maps in their heads. He jumped onto the sidewalk as nimbly as a goat, then turned his dark glasses back in my direction. There was an expression of crazed triumph on his tear-streaked face, and the dark lenses looked more like holes than ever. Big ones, as if someone had hit him with two large-caliber shotgun rounds.

"Blondie's is gone, I toldja!" he screamed. *"My mom says he upped and ran away with that redhead floozy he hired last month! You should be so lucky, you ugly prick!"*

He turned and went running up Sunset in that strange way of his, with his splayed fingers held out in front of him. People stood in little clusters on both sides of the street, looking at him, looking at the papers fluttering in the street, looking at me.

Mostly looking at me, it seemed.

This time Peoria—well, okay, Francis—made it as far as Derringer's Bar before turning to deliver one final salvo.

"Fuck you, Mr. Umney!" he screamed, and ran on.

II. Vernon's Cough.

I managed to pull myself erect and make my way across
the street. Peoria, aka Francis Smith, was long gone, but
I wanted to put those blowing newspapers behind me, too.
Looking at them was giving me a headache that was
somehow worse than the ache in my groin.

On the far side of the street I stared into Felt's Station-
ery as if the new Parker ball-point pen in the window was
the most fascinating thing I'd ever seen in my life (or
maybe it was those sexy imitation-leather appointment
books). After five minutes or so—time enough to commit
every item in the dusty show-window to memory—I felt
capable of resuming my interrupted voyage up Sunset
without listening too noticeably to port.

Questions circled in my mind the way mosquitoes circled your head at the drive-in in San Pedro when you forget to bring along an insect stick or two. I was able to
ignore most of them, but a couple got through. First,
what the hell had gotten into Peoria? Second, what the
hell had gotten into me? I kept slapping at these uncom-

fortable queries until I got to Blondie's City Eats, Open 24 Hrs, Bagels Our Specialty, on the corner of Sunset and Travernia, and when I got that far, they were driven out in a single wallop. Blondie's had been on that corner for as long as I could remember—the sharpies and the hustlers and the hipsters and the hypes going in and going out, not to mention the debs, the dykes, and the dopes. A famous silent-movie star was once arrested for murder as he was coming out of Blondie's, and I myself had concluded a nasty piece of business there not so long ago, shooting a coked-up fashion-plate named Dunninger who had killed three hopheads in the aftermath of a Hollywood dope party. It was also the place where I'd said goodbye to the silver-haired, violet-eyed Ardis McGill. I'd spent the rest of that lost night walking in a rare Los Angeles fog which might have only been behind my eyes . . . and trickling down my cheeks, by the time the sun came up.

Blondie's closed? Blondie's gone? Impossible, you would have said—more likely that the Statue of Liberty should have disappeared from her barren lick of rock in New York Harbor.

Impossible but true. The window which had once held a mouth-watering selection of pies and cakes was soaped over, but the job had been done indifferently, and I could see a nearly empty room through the stripes. The lino looked filthy and barren. The grease-darkened blades of the overhead fans hung down like the propellers of crashed airplanes. There were a few tables left, and six or eight of the familiar red-upholstered chairs piled on them with the legs sticking up, but that was all ... except for a couple of empty sugar-shakers tumbled in one corner.

I stood there trying to get it into my head, and it was like trying to get a big sofa up a narrow flight of stairs. All that life and excitement, all that late-night hustle and surprise—how could it be ended? It didn't seem like a mistake; it seemed like a blasphemy. For me Blondie's had summed up all the glittering contradictions that surrounded L.A.'s essentially dark and loveless heart; I had sometimes thought Blondie's *was* L.A. as I had known it over the last fifteen or twenty years, only drawn small. Where else could you see a mobster eating breakfast at 9:00 P.M. with a priest, or a diamond-decked glamorpuss sitting on a counter-stool next to a grease-monkey celebrating the end of his shift with a hot cup of java? I suddenly found myself thinking of the Cuban bandleader and his heart attack again, this time with considerably more sympathy.

All that fabulous starry City of Lost Angels *life*—do you get it, chum? Are you picking up this newsflash?

The sign hung in the door read CLOSED FOR RENOVATIONS, REOPENING SOON, but I didn't believe it. Empty sugar-shakers lying in the corner do not, in my experience, indicate renovations in progress. Peoria had been right: Blondie's was history. I turned away and went on up the street, but now I walked slowly and had to consciously order my head to stay up. As I approached the Fulwider Building, where I've kept an office for more years than I like to think about, an odd certainty gripped me. The handles of the big double doors would be wrapped up in a thick tow-chain and held with a padlock. The glass would be soaped over in indifferent stripes. And there would be a sign reading CLOSED FOR RENOVATIONS, REOPENING SOON.

By the time I reached the building, this nutty idea had taken over my mind with the force of a compulsion, and not even the sight of Bill Tuggle, the rummy CPA from the third floor, going inside could quite dispel it. But seeing is believing, they say, and when I got to 2221, I saw no chain, no sign, and no soap on the glass. It was just the Fulwider, the same as ever. I went into the lobby, smelled the familiar odor—it reminds me of the pink cakes they put in the urinals of public men's rooms these days—and glanced around at the same ratty palm trees overhanging the same faded red tile floor.

Bill was standing next to Vernon Klein, world's oldest elevator operator, in Car 2. In his frayed red suit and ancient pillbox hat, Vernon looks like a cross between the Philip Morris bellboy and a rhesus monkey which has fallen into an industrial steam-cleaning machine. He looked up at me with his mournful basset-hound eyes, which were watering from the Camel pasted in the middle of his mouth. His peepers should have gotten used to the smoke years ago; I couldn't remember ever having seen him without a Camel parked in that same position.

Bill moved over a little, but not far enough. There wasn't room enough in the car for him to move far enough. I'm not sure there would have been room in Rhode Island for him to move far enough. Delaware, maybe. He smelled like bologna which has spent a year or so marinating in cheap bourbon. And just when I thought it couldn't get any worse, he belched.

"Sorry, Clyde."

"Well, you certainly ought to be," I said, waving the air in front of my face as Vern slid the gate across the front of the car and prepared to fly us to the moon . . . or at least to the seventh floor. "What drainpipe did you spend the night in, Bill?"

Yet there was something comforting about that smell— I'd be lying if I said there wasn't. Because it was a *famil-*

iar smell. It was just Bill Tuggle, odoriferous, hung over, and standing with his knees slightly bent, as if someone had filled the crotch of his underpants with chicken salad and he'd just realized it. Not pleasant, nothing about that morning's elevator ride was pleasant, but it was at least *known*.

Bill gave me a sick smile as the elevator began to rattle upward but said nothing.

I swung my head in Vernon's direction, mostly to get away from the smell of overbaked accountant, but whatever small talk I'd been meaning to make died in my throat. The two pictures which had hung over Vern's stool since the beginning of time—one of Jesus walking on the Sea of Galilee while his boatbound disciples gawped at him and the other of Vern's wife in a buckskin-fringed Sweetheart of the Rodeo outfit and a turn-of-the-century hairdo—were both gone. What had replaced them shouldn't have been shocking, especially in light of Vernon's age, but it hit me like a barge-load of bricks just the same.

It was a card, that's all—a simple card showing the silhouette of a man fishing on a lake at sunset. It was the sentiment printed below the canoe that floored me: HAPPY RETIREMENT!

You could have doubled the way I felt when Peoria told

me he might see again and still have come up short. Memories flickered through my mind with the speed of cards being shuffled by a riverboat gambler. There was the time Vern broke into the office next to mine to call an ambulance when that nutty dame, Agnes Sternwood, first tore my phone out of the wall and then swallowed what she swore was drain-clear. The "drain-cleaner" turned out to be nothing but crystals of raw sugar, and the office Vern broke into turned out to be a high-class horse parlor. So far as I know, the guy who leased the place and slapped MacKenzie Imports on the door is still receiving his annual Sears Roebuck catalog in San Quentin. Then there was the guy Vern cold-conked with his stool just before he could ventilate my guts; that was the Mavis Weld business again, of course. Not to mention the time he brought his daughter to me—what a babe *she* was!— when she got involved with that dirty-picture racket.

Vern retiring?

It wasn't possible. It just wasn't.

"Vernon," I asked, "what kind of joke is this?"

"No joke, Mr. Umney," he said, and as he brought the elevator car to a stop on Three, he began to hack a deep cough I'd never heard in all the years I'd known him. It was like listening to marble bowling balls rolling down a stone alley. He took the Camel out of his mouth, and I was horrified to see the end of it was pink, and not with lipstick. He looked at it for a moment, grimaced, then replaced it and yanked back the accordion grille. *"Thuh-ree,* Mr. Tuggle."

"Thanks, Vern," Bill said.

"Remember the party on Friday," Vernon said. His words were muffled; he'd taken a handkerchief spotted with brown stains out of his back pocket and was wiping his lips with it. "I sure would admire for you to come." He glanced at me with his rheumy eyes, and what was in them scared the bejabbers out of me. Something was waiting for Vernon Klein just around the next bend in the road, and that look said Vernon knew all about it. "You too, Mr. Umney—we been through a lot together, and I'd be tickled to raise a glass with you."

"Wait a minute!" I shouted, grabbing Bill as he tried to step out of the elevator. "You wait just a God damned minute, both of you! *What* party? What's going on here?"

"Retirement," Bill said. "It usually happens at some point after your hair turns white, in case you've been too busy to notice. Vernon's party is going to be in the basement on Friday afternoon. Everybody in the building's going to be there, and I'm going to make my world-famous Dynamite Punch. What's the matter with you,

Clyde? You've known for a month that Vern was finishing up on May thirtieth."

That made me angry all over again, the way I'd been when Peoria called me a faggot. I grabbed Bill by the padded shoulders of his double-breasted suit and gave him a shake. "The hell you say!"

He gave me a small, pained smile. "The hell I don't, Clyde. But if you don't want to come, fine. Stay away. You've been acting *poco loco* for the last six months, anyhow."

I shook him again. "What do you mean, *poco loco?*"

"Crazy as a loon, nutty as a fruitcake, two wheels off the road, out to lunch, playing without a full deck—any of those ring a bell? And before you answer, just let me inform you that if you shake me one more time, even a *little* shake, my guts are going to explode straight out through my chest, and not even dry-cleaning will get *that* mess off your suit."

He pulled away before I could do it again even if I'd wanted to and started down the hall with the seat of his pants hanging somewhere down around the level of his knees, as per usual. He glanced back just once, while Vernon was sliding the brass gate across. "You need to take some time off, Clyde. Starting last week."

"What's gotten into you?" I shouted at him. "What's

gotten into *all* of you?" But by then the inner door was closed and we were headed up again—this time to Seven. My little slice of heaven. Vern dropped his cigarette butt into the bucket of sand that squats in the corner, and immediately stuck a fresh one in his kisser. He popped a wooden match alight with his thumbnail, set the fag on fire, and immediately started coughing again. Now I could see fine drops of blood misting out from between his cracked lips. It was a gruesome sight. His eyes had dropped; they stared vacantly into the far corner, seeing nothing, hoping for nothing. Bill Tuggle's B.O. hung between us like the Ghost of Binges Past.

"Okay, Vern," I said. "What is it and where are you going?"

Vernon had never been one to wear out the English language, and that at least hadn't changed. "It's Big C," he said. "On Saturday I catch the Desert Blossom to Arizona. I'm going to live with my sister. I don't expect to wear out my welcome, though. She might have to change the bed twice." He brought the elevator to a stop and rattled the gate back. "*Seven*, Mr. Umney. Your little slice of heaven." He smiled at that just as he always did, but this time it looked like the kind of smile you see on the candy skulls down in Tijuana, on the Day of the Dead.

Now that the elevator door was open, I smelled something up here in my little slice of heaven that was so out of place it took a moment for me to recognize it: fresh paint. Once it was noted, I filed it. I had other fish to fry.

"This isn't right," I said. "You know it isn't, Vern."

He turned his frightening vacant eyes on me. Death in them, a black shape flapping and beckoning just beyond the faded blue. "What isn't right, Mr. Umney?"

"You're supposed to be *here*, damn it! Right *here!* Sitting on your stool with Jesus and your wife over your head. Not *this!*" I reached up, grabbed the card with the picture of the man fishing on the lake, tore it in two, put the pieces together, tore it in four, and then gave them the toss. They fluttered to the faded red rug on the floor of the elevator car like confetti.

"S'posed to be right here," he repeated, those terrible eyes of his never leaving mine. Beyond us, two men in paint-splattered overalls had turned to look in our direction.

"That's right."

"For how long, Mr. Umney? Since you know everything else, you can probably tell me that, can'tcha? How long am I supposed to keep drivin this damned car?"

"Well . . . forever," I said, and the word hung between us, another ghost in the cigarette-smokey elevator car. Given a choice of ghosts, I guess I would have picked Bill

Tuggle's B.O. . . . but I wasn't given a choice. Instead, I said it again. "Forever, Vern."

He dragged on his Camel, coughed out smoke and a fine spray of blood, and went on looking at me. "It ain't my place to give the tenants advice, Mr. Umney, but I guess I'll give you some, anyway—it being my last week and all. You might consider seeing a doctor. The kind that shows you ink-pitchers and you say what they look like."

"You can't retire, Vern." My heart was beating harder than ever, but I managed to keep my voice level. "You just can't."

"No?" He took his cigarette out of his mouth—fresh blood was already soaking into the tip—and then looked back at me. His smile was ghastly. "The way it looks to me, I ain't exactly got a choice, Mr. Umney."

III. Of Painters and Pesos.

The smell of fresh paint seared my nose, overpowering both the smell of Vernon's smoke and Bill Tuggle's armpits. The men in the coveralls were currently taking up space not far from my office door. They had put down a dropcloth, and the tools of their trade were spread out all along it—tins and brushes and turp. There were two step-ladders as well, flanking the painters like scrawny bookends. What I wanted to do was to run down the hall, kicking the whole works every whichway as I went. What right had they to paint these old dark walls that glaring, sacrilegious white?

Instead, I walked up to the one who looked as if it might take a two-digit number to express his IQ and politely asked what he and his fellow mug thought they were doing. He glanced around at me. "Hellzit look like? I'm givin Miss America a finger-frig and Chick there's putting rouge on Betty Grable's nippy-nips."

I'd had enough. Enough of them, enough of everything. I reached out, grabbed the quiz-kid under the armpit, and

26

used my fingertips to engage a particularly nasty nerve that hides up there. He screamed and dropped his brush. White paint splattered his shoes. His partner gave me a timid doe-eyed look and took a step backward.

"If you try taking off before I'm done with you," I snarled, "you're going to find the handle of your paint-brush so far up your ass you'll need a boathook to find the bristles. You want to try me and see if I'm lying?"

He stopped moving and just stood there on the edge of the dropcloth, eyes darting from side to side, looking for help. There was none to be had. I half-expected Candy to open my door and look out to see what the fracas was, but the door stayed firmly closed. I turned my attention back to the quiz-kid I was holding onto.

"The question was simple enough, bud—what the hell are you doing here? Can you answer it, or do I give you another blast?"

I twiddled my fingers in his armpit just to refresh his memory and he screamed again. *"Paintin the hall! Jeezis, can't you see?"*

I could see, all right, and even if I'd been blind, I could *smell*. I hated what both of those senses were telling me. The hallway wasn't *supposed* to be painted, especially not this glaring, light-reflecting white. It was supposed to be dim and shadowy; it was supposed to smell like dust and old memories. Whatever had started with the Demmicks' unaccustomed silence was getting worse all the time. I was mad as hell, as this unfortunate fellow was discovering. I was also scared, but that was a feeling you get good at hiding when carrying a heater in a clamshell holster is part of the way you make your living.

"Who sent you two dubs down here?"

"Our *boss*," he said, looking at me as if I were crazy. "We work for Challis Custom Painters, on Van Nuys. The boss is Hap Corrigan. If you want to know who hired the cump'ny, you'll have to ask h—"

"It was the owner," the other painter said quietly. "The owner of this building. A guy named Samuel Landry."

I searched my memory, trying to put the name of Samuel Landry together with what I knew of the Fulwider Building and couldn't do it. In fact, I couldn't put the name of Samuel Landry together with anything . . . yet for all that it seemed almost to chime in my head, like a church-bell you can hear from miles away on a foggy morning.

"You're lying," I said, but with no real force. I said it simply because it was something to say.

"Call the boss," the other painter said. Appearances could be deceiving; he was apparently the brighter of the two, after all. He reached inside his grimy, paint-smeared coverall and brought out a little card.

I waved it away, suddenly tired. "Who in the name of Christ would want to paint this place, anyway?"

It wasn't them I was asking, but the painter who'd offered me the business card answered just the same. "Well, it brightens the place up," he said cautiously. "You gotta admit that."

"Son," I asked, taking a step toward him, "did your mother ever have any kids that lived, or did she just produce the occasional afterbirth like you?"

"Hey, whatever, whatever," he said, taking a step backward. I followed his worried gaze down to my own balled-up fists and forced them open again. He didn't look very relieved, and I actually didn't blame him very much. "You don't like it—you're coming through loud and clear on that score. But I gotta do what the boss tells me, don't I? I mean, hell, that's the American way."

He glanced at his partner, then back to me. It was a quick glance, really no more than a flick, but in my line of work I'd seen it more than once, and it's the kind of look you file away. *Don't bother this guy,* it said. *Don't bump him, don't rattle him. He's nitro.*

"I mean, I've got a wife and a little kid to take care of,"

he went on. "There's a Depression going on out there, you know."

Confusion came over me then, drowning my anger the way a downpour drowns a brushfire. *Was* there a Depression going on out there? Was there?

"I know," I said, not knowing anything. "Let's just forget it, what do you say?"

"Sure," the painters agreed, so eager they sounded like half of a barbershop quartet. The one I'd mistakenly tabbed as half-bright had his left hand buried deep in his right armpit, trying to get that nerve to go back to sleep. I could have told him he had an hour's work ahead of him, maybe more, but I didn't want to talk to them anymore. I didn't want to talk to anyone or see anyone—not even the delectable Candy Kane, whose humid glances and smooth, subtropical curves have been known to send seasoned street-brawlers reeling to their knees. The only thing I wanted to do was to get across the outer office and into my inner sanctum. There was a bottle of Robb's Rye in the bottom lefthand drawer, and right now I needed a shot in the worst way.

I walked down toward the frosted-glass door marked CLYDE UMNEY PRIVATE INVESTIGATOR, restraining a renewed urge to see if I could drop-kick a can of Dutch Boy Oyster White through the window at the end of the hall and out onto the fire-escape. I was actually reaching for my doorknob when a thought struck me and I turned back to the painters . . . but slowly, so they wouldn't believe I was being gripped by some new seizure. Also, I had an idea that if I turned too fast, I'd see them grinning at each other and twirling their fingers around their ears—the looney-gesture we all learned in the schoolyard.

They weren't twirling their fingers, but they hadn't taken their eyes off me, either. The half-smart one seemed to be gauging the distance to the door marked STAIRWELL. Suddenly I wanted to tell them that I wasn't such a bad guy when you got to know me; that there were, in fact, a few clients and at least one ex-wife who thought me something of a hero. But that wasn't a thing you could say about yourself, especially not to a couple of bozos like these.

"Take it easy," I said. "I'm not going to jump you. I just wanted to ask another question."

They relaxed a little. A very little, actually.

"Ask it," Painter Number Two said.

"Either of you ever played the numbers down in Tijuana?"

"*La lotería?*" Number One asked.

"Your knowledge of Spanish stuns me. Yeah. *La lotería.*"

Number One shook his head. "Mex numbers and Mex call houses are strictly for suckers."

Why do you think I asked you? I thought but didn't say.

"Besides," he went on, "you win ten or twenty thousand pesos, big deal. What's that in real money? Fifty bucks? Eighty?"

My mom hit the lottery down in Tijuana, Peoria had said, and I had known something about it wasn't right even then. *Forty thousand bucks ... My Uncle Fred went down and picked up the cash yest'y afternoon. He brought it back in the saddlebag of his Vinnie!*

"Yeah," I said, "something like that, I guess. And they always pay off that way, don't they? In pesos?"

He gave me that look again, as if I was crazy, then remembered I really was and readjusted his face. "Well, yeah. It *is* the Mexican lottery, you know. They couldn't very well pay off in dollars."

"How true," I said, and in my mind I saw Peoria's thin, eager face, heard him saying, *It was spread all over my mom's bed! Forty-froggin-thousand smackers!*

Except how could a blind kid be sure of the exact amount ... or even that it really was money he was rolling around in? The answer was simple: he couldn't. But even a blind newsboy would know that *la lotería* paid off in pesos rather than in dollars, and even a blind news-boy had to know you couldn't carry forty thousand dollars' worth of Mexican lettuce in the saddlebag of a Vincent motorcycle. His uncle would have needed a City of Los Angeles dump truck to transport that much dough.

Confusion, confusion—nothing but dark clouds of confusion.

"Thanks," I said, and headed for my office.

I'm sure that was a relief for all three of us.

IV. Umney's Last Client.

"Candy, honey, I don't want to see anybody or take any ca—"

I broke off. The outer office was empty. Candy's desk in the corner was unnaturally bare, and after a moment I saw why: the IN/OUT tray had been dumped into the trash basket and her pictures of Errol Flynn and William Powell were both gone. So was her Philco. The little blue stenographer's stool, from which Candy had been wont to flash her gorgeous games, was unoccupied.

My eyes returned to the IN/OUT tray sticking out of the trash can like the prow of a sinking ship, and for a moment my heart leaped. Perhaps someone had been in here, tossed the place, kidnapped Candy. Perhaps it was a case, in other words. At that moment I would have welcomed a case, even if it meant some mug was tying Candy up at this very moment . . . and adjusting the rope over the firm swell of her breasts with particular care. Any way out of the cobwebs that seemed to be falling around me sounded just peachy to me.

The trouble with the idea was simple; the room hadn't been tossed. The IN/OUT was in the trash, true enough, but that didn't indicate a struggle; in fact, it was more as if . . .

There was just one thing left on the desk, placed squarely in the center of the blotter. A white envelope. Just looking at it gave me a bad feeling. My feet carried me across the room just the same, however, and I picked it up. Seeing my name written across the front of the envelope in Candy's wide loops and swirls was no surprise; it was just another unpleasant part of this long, unpleasant morning.

I ripped it open and a single slip of note-paper fell out into my hand.

Dear Clyde,

I have had all of the groping and sneering I'm going to take from you, and I am tired of your ridiculous and childish jokes about my name. Life is too short to be pawed by a middle-aged divorce detective with bad breath. You did have your good points Clyde but they are getting drownded out by the bad ones, especially since you started drinking all the time.

Do yourself a favor and grow up.

Yours truly,
Arlene Cain

P.S.: I'm going back to my mother's in Idaho. Do not try to get in touch with me.

I held the note a moment or two longer, looking at it unbelievingly, then dropped it. One phrase from it recurred as I watched it seesaw lazily down toward the already occupied trash basket: *I am tired of your ridiculous and childish jokes about my name.* But had I ever known her name was anything *other* than Candy Kane? I searched my mind as the note continued its lazy—and seemingly endless—swoops back and forth, and the answer was an honest and resounding no. Her name had *always* been Candy Kane, we'd joked about it many a time, and if we'd had a few rounds of office slap-and-tickle, what of that? She'd always enjoyed it. We both had.

Did she enjoy it? a voice spoke up from somewhere deep inside me. *Did she really, or is that just another little fairytale you've been telling yourself all these years?*

I tried to shut that voice out, and after a moment or two I succeeded, but the one that replaced it was even worse. That voice belonged to none other than Peoria Smith. *I can quit actin like I died and went to heaven every time some blowhard leaves me a nickle tip*, he said. *Ain't you picking up on this newsflash, Mr. Umney?*

"Shut up, kid," I said to the empty room. "Gabriel Heatter you ain't." I turned away from Candy's desk and as I did, faces passed in front of my mind's eye like the faces of some lunatic marching band from hell: George

36

and Gloria Demmick, Peoria Smith, Bill Tuggle, Vernon Klein, a million-dollar blonde who went under the two-bit name of Arlene Cain . . . even the two painters were there.

Confusion, confusion, nothing but confusion.

Head down, I trudged into my office, closed the door behind me, and sat at the desk. Dimly, through the closed window, I could hear the traffic out on Sunset. I had an idea that, for the right person, it was still a spring morning so L.A.-perfect you expected to see the little trademark symbol stamped on it somewhere, but for me all the light had gone from the day . . . inside as well as out. I thought about the bottle of hooch in the bottom drawer, but all of a sudden even bending down to get it seemed like too much work. It seemed, in fact, a job akin to climbing Mount Everest in tennis shoes.

The smell of fresh paint had penetrated all the way into my inner sanctum. It was a smell I ordinarily liked, but not then. At that moment it was the smell of everything that had gone wrong since the Demmicks hadn't come into their Hollywood bungalow bouncing wisecracks off each other like rubber balls and playing their records at top volume and throwing their Corgi into conniptions with their endless billing and cooing. It occurred to me with perfect clarity and simplicity—the way I'd always imagined great truths must occur to the people they occur to—that if some doctor could cut out the cancer that was killing the Fulwider Building's elevator operator, it would be white. *Oyster* white. And it would smell just like fresh Dutch Boy paint.

This thought was so tiring that I had to put my head down with the heels of my palms pressed against my temples, holding it in place . . . or maybe just keeping what was inside from exploding out and making a mess on the walls. And when the door opened softly and footsteps entered the room, I didn't look up. It seemed like more of an effort than I was able to make at that particular moment.

Besides, I had the strange idea that I already *knew* who it was. I couldn't put a name to my knowledge, but the step was somehow familiar. So was the cologne, although I knew I wouldn't be able to name it even if someone had put a gun to my head, and for a very simple reason: I'd never smelled it before in my life. How could I recognize a scent I'd never smelled before, you ask? I can't answer that one, bud, but I did.

Nor was that the worst of it. The worst of it was this: I was scared nearly out of my mind. I've faced blazing guns in the hands of angry men, which is bad, and daggers in the hands of angry women, which is a thousand times worse; I was once tied to the wheel of a Packard automobile that had been parked on the tracks of a busy freight line; I have even been tossed out a third-story window. It's been an eventful life, all right, but nothing in it had ever scared me the way the smell of that cologne and that soft footstep scared me.

My head seemed to weigh at least six hundred pounds.

"Clyde," a voice said. A voice I'd never heard before, a voice I nevertheless knew as well as my own. Just that one word and the weight of my head went up to an even ton.

"Get outta here, whoever you are," I said without looking up. "Joint's closed." And something made me add, "For renovations."

"Bad day, Clyde?"

Was there sympathy in that voice? I thought maybe there was, and somehow that made things worse. Whoever this mug was, I didn't want his sympathy. Something told me that his sympathy would be more dangerous than his hate.

"Not so bad," I said, supporting my heavy, aching head with the palms of my hands and looking down at my desk-blotter for all I was worth. Written in the upper lefthand corner was Mavis Weld's number. I sent my eyes tracing over it again and again—BEverley 6-4214. Keeping my eyes on the blotter seemed like a good idea. I didn't know who my visitor was, but I knew I didn't want to see him. Right then it was the only thing I *did* know.

"I think maybe you're being a little . . . disingenuous, shall we say?" the voice asked, and it was sympathy, all right; the sound of it made my stomach curl up into something that felt like a quivering fist soaked with acid. There was a creak as he dropped into the client's chair.

"I don't exactly know what that word means, but by all means, let's say it," I agreed. "And now that we have, why don't you rise up righteous, Moggins, and shift on out of here. I'm thinking of taking a sick day. I can do that without much argument, you see, because I'm the boss. Neat, the way things work out sometimes, isn't it?"

"I suppose so. Look at me, Clyde."

My heart stuttered but my head stayed down and my eyes kept tracing over BEverley 6-4214. Part of me wondered if hell was hot enough for Mavis Weld. When I spoke, my voice came out steady. I was surprised but grateful. "In fact, I might take a whole year of sick days. In Carmel, maybe. Sit out on the deck with the *American Mercury* in my lap and watch the big ones come in from Hawaii."

"Look at me."

I didn't want to, but my head came up just the same.

He was sitting in the client's chair where Mavis had once sat, and Ardis McGill, and Big Tom Hatfield. Even Vernon Klein had sat there once, when he got those pictures of his daughter wearing nothing but an opium grin and her birthday suit. Sitting there with the same patch of California sun slanting across his features—features I most certainly *had* seen before. The last time had been less than an hour ago, in my bathroom mirror. I'd been scraping a Gillette Blue Blade over them.

The expression of sympathy in his eyes—in *my* eyes—was the most hideous thing I'd ever seen, and when he held out his hand—held out *my* hand—I felt a sudden urge to wheel around in my swivel chair, get to my feet, and go running straight out my seventh-floor office window. I think I might even have done it, if I hadn't been so confused, so totally lost. I've read the word *unmanned* plenty of times—it's a favorite of the pulpsmiths and sobsisters—but this was the first time I'd ever actually felt that way.

Suddenly the office darkened. The day had been perfectly clear, I would have sworn to that, but a cloud had crossed the sun just the same. The man on the other side of the desk was at least ten years older than I was, maybe fifteen, his hair almost completely white while mine was still almost all black, but that didn't change the simple fact—no matter what he was calling himself or how old he looked, he was me. Had I thought his voice sounded familiar? Sure. The way your own voice sounds familiar—although not quite the way it sounds inside your own head—when you hear it on a recording.

He picked my limp hand up off the desk, shook it with the briskness of a real-estate agent on the make, then dropped it again. It hit the desk-blotter with a plop, landing on Mavis Weld's telephone number. When I raised my fingers, I saw that Mavis's number was gone. In fact, *all* the numbers I'd scratched on the blotter over the years were gone. It was as clear as . . . well, as clear as a hardshell Baptist's conscience.

"Jesus," I croaked. "Jesus Christ."

"Not at all," the older version of me sitting in the client's chair on the other side of the desk said. "Landry, Samauel D. Landry. At your service."

V. An Interview with God.

Even as rattled as I was, it only took me two or three seconds to place the name, probably because I'd heard it such a short time ago. According to Painter Number Two, Samuel Landry was the reason why the long dark hall leading to my office was soon going to be oyster white. Landry was the owner of the Fulwider Building.

A crazy idea suddenly occurred to me, but its patent craziness did nothing to dim the sudden blaze of hope which accompanied it. They—whoever *they* are—say that everyone on the face of the earth has a double. Maybe Landry was mine. Maybe we were identical twins, unrelated doubles who had somehow been born to different parents and ten or fifteen years out of step in time with each other. The idea did nothing to explain the rest of the day's high weirdness, but it was something to hang onto, damn it.

"What can I do for you, Mr. Landry?" I asked. I was trying like hell, but my voice was no longer quite steady. "If it's about the lease, you'll have to give me a day or two

43

to get squared around. It seems my secretary just discovered she had pressing business back home in Armpit, Idaho."

Landry paid absolutely no attention to this feeble effort on my part to shift the focus of the conversation. "Yes," he said in a musing tone of voice, "I imagine it's been the granddaddy of bad days ... and it's my fault. I'm sorry, Clyde—really. Meeting you in person has been ... well, not what I expected. Not at all. For one thing, I like you quite a bit better than I expected to. But there's no going back now." And he fetched a deep sigh. I didn't like the sound of it very much.

"What do you mean by that?" My voice was trembling worse than ever now, and the blaze of hope was dying. Lack of oxygen inside the cave-in site which had once been my brain seemed to be the cause.

He didn't answer right away. He leaned over instead, and grasped the handle of the slim leather case leaning against the front leg of the client's chair. The initials stamped on it were S.D.L., and I deduced that my weird visitor had brought it in with him. I didn't win the Shamus of the Year Award in 1934 and '35 for nothing, you know.

I had never seen a case quite like it in my life—it was too small and too slim to be a briefcase, and it was fastened not with buckles and straps but with a zipper. I'd never seen a zipper quite like this one, either, now that I thought about it. The teeth were extremely tiny, and they hardly looked like metal at all.

But the oddities only *began* with Landry's luggage. Even setting aside his uncanny older-brother resemblance to me, Landry looked like no businessman I'd ever seen in my life, and certainly not one prosperous enough to own the Fulwider Building. It's not the Ritz, granted, but it *is* in downtown L.A., and my client (if that was what he was) looked like an Okie on a good day, one which had included a bath and a shave.

He was wearing blue jeans pants, for one thing, and a pair of sneakers on his feet . . . except they didn't look like any sneakers I'd ever seen before. They were great big clumpy things. What they *really* looked like were the shoes Boris Karloff wears as part of his Frankenstein get-up, and if they were made of canvas, I'd eat my favorite Fedora. The word written up the sides in red script looked like the name of a dish on a Chinese carry-out menu: REEBOK.

I looked down at the blotter which had once been covered with a tangle of telephone numbers, and suddenly realized that I could no longer remember Mavis Weld's, although I must have called it a billion times only this past winter. That feeling of dread intensified.

"Mister," I said, "I wish you'd state your business and get out of here. Come to think of it, why don't you skip the talking and just go right to the getting-out part?"

He smiled ... tiredly, I thought. That was the other thing. The face above the plain open-collared white shirt looked terribly tired. Terribly sad, as well. It said the man who owned it had been through things I couldn't even dream of. I felt some sympathy for my visitor, but what I mostly felt was fear. And anger. Because it was *my* face, too, and the bastard had apparently gone a long way toward wearing it out.

"Sorry, Clyde," he said. "No can do."

He put his hand on that tiny, cunning zipper, and all at once Landry opening that case was the last thing in the world I wanted. To stop him I said, "Do you always go visiting your tenants dressed like a guy who makes his living following the cabbage crop? What are you, one of those eccentric millionaires?"

"I'm eccentric, all right," he said. "And it won't do you any good to draw this business out, Clyde."

"What gave you that ide—"

Then he said the thing I'd been dreading, and put out

the last tiny flicker of hope at the same time. "I know *all* your ideas, Clyde. After all, I'm *you."*

I licked my lips and forced myself to speak; anything to keep him from yanking that zipper. Anything at all. My voice came out husky, but at least it *did* come out.

"Yeah, I noticed the resemblance. I'm not familiar with the cologne, though. I'm an Old Spice man, myself."

His thumb and finger remained pinched on the zipper, but he didn't pull it. At least not yet.

"But you like this," he said with perfect assurance, "and you'd use it if you could get it down at the Rexall on the corner, wouldn't you? Unfortunately, you can't. It's Aramis, and it won't be invented for another forty years or so." He glanced down at his weird, ugly basketball shoes. "Like my sneakers."

"The devil you say."

"Well, yes, I suppose the devil might come into it somewhere," Landry said, and he didn't smile.

"Where are you from?"

"I thought you knew." Landry pulled the zipper, revealing a rectangular gadget made of some smooth plastic. It was the same color the seventh-floor hall was going to be by the time the sun went down. I'd never seen anything like it. There was no brand name on it, just something that must have been a serial number: T-1000.

47

Landry lifted it out of its carrying case, thumbed the catches on the sides, and lifted the hinged top to reveal something that looked like the telescreen in a Buck Rogers movie. "I come from the future," Landry said. "Just like in a pulp magazine story."

"You come from Sunnyland Sanitarium, more like it," I croaked.

"But not *exactly* like a pulp science-fiction story," he went on, ignoring what I'd said. "No, not exactly." He pushed a button on the side of the plastic case. There was a faint whirring sound from inside the gadget, followed by a brief, whistling beep. The thing sitting on his lap looked like some strange stenographer's machine . . . and I had an idea that that wasn't far from the truth.

He looked up at me and said, "What was your father's name, Clyde?"

I looked at him for a moment, resisting an urge to lick my lips again. The room was still dark, the sun still behind some cloud that hadn't even been in sight when I came in off the street. Landry's face seemed to float in the gloom like an old, shrivelled balloon.

"What's that got to do with the price of cucumbers in Monrovia?" I asked.

"You don't know, do you?"

"Of course I do," I said, and I did. I just couldn't come

up with it, that was all—it was stuck there on the tip of my tongue, like Mavis Weld's phone number, which had been BAyshore something-or-other.

"How about your mother's?"

"Quit playing games with me!"

"Here's an easy one—what high school did you go to? Every red-blooded American man remembers what school he went to, right? Or the first girl he ever went all the way with. Or the town he grew up in. Was yours San Luis Obispo?"

I opened my mouth, but this time nothing came out.

"Carmel?"

That sounded right . . . and then felt all wrong. My head was whirling.

"Or maybe it was Dusty Bottom, New Mexico."

"Cut the crap!" I shouted.

"Do you know? *Do* you?"

"Yes! It was—"

He bent over. Rattled the keys of his strange steno machine.

"San Diego! Born and raised!"

He put the machine on my desk and turned it around so I could read the words floating in the window above the keyboard.

My eyes dropped from the window to the word stamped into the plastic frame surrounding it.

"What's a Toshiba?" I asked. "Something that comes on the side when you order a Reebok dinner?"

"It's a Japanese electronics company."

I laughed dryly. "Who're you kidding, mister? The Japs can't even make wind-up toys without getting the springs in upside down."

"Not now," he agreed, "and speaking of now, Clyde, when *is* now? What year is it?"

"1938," I said, then raised a half-numb hand to my face and rubbed my lips. "Wait a minute—1939."

"It might even be 1940. Am I right?"

I said nothing, but I felt my face heating up.

"Don't feel bad, Clyde; you don't know because *I* don't know. I always left it vague. The time-frame I was trying for was actually more of a *feel* . . . call it Chandler American Time, if you like. It worked like gangbusters for most of my readers, and it made things simpler from a copy-editing standpoint as well, because you can never exactly pinpoint the passage of time. Haven't you ever noticed how often you say things like 'for more years than I can

50

remember' or 'longer ago than I like to think about' or 'since Hector was a pup'?"

"Nope—can't say that I have." But now that he mentioned it, I *did* notice. And that made me think of the *L.A. Times*. I read it every day, but exactly which days were they? You couldn't tell from the paper itself, because there was never a date on the masthead, only that slogan which reads "America's Fairest Newspaper in America's Fairest City."

"You say those things because time doesn't really pass in this world. It is . . ." He paused, then smiled. It was a terrible thing to look at, that smile, full of yearning and strange greed. "It is one of its many charms," he finished.

I was scared, but I've always been able to bite the bullet when I felt it really needed biting, and this was one of those times. "Tell me what the hell's going on here."

"All right . . . but you're already beginning to know, Clyde. Aren't you?"

"Maybe. I don't know my dad's name or my mom's name or the name of the first girl I ever went to bed with because *you* don't know them. Is that it?"

He nodded, smiling the way a teacher would smile at a pupil who's made a leap of logic and come up with the right answer against all odds. But his eyes were full of that terrible sympathy.

"And when you wrote San Diego on your gadget there and it came into my head at the same time . . ."

He nodded, encouraging me.

"It isn't just the Fulwider Building you own, is it?" I swallowed, trying to get rid of a large blockage in my throat that had no intention of going anywhere. "You own everything."

But Landry was shaking his head. "Not *everything*. Just Los Angeles and a few surrounding areas. This version of Los Angeles, that is, complete with the occasional continuity glitch or made-up addition."

"Bull," I said, but I whispered the word.

"See the picture on the wall to the left of the door, Clyde?"

I glanced at it, but hardly had to; it was Washington crossing the Delaware, and it had been there since . . . well, since Hector was a pup.

Landry had taken his plastic Buck Rogers steno machine back onto his lap, and was bending over it.

"Don't do that!" I shouted, and tried to reach for him. I couldn't do it. My arms had no strength, it seemed, and I could summon no resolve. I felt lethargic, drained, as if I had lost about three pints of blood and was losing more all the time.

He rattled the keys again. Turned the machine toward

me so I could read the words in the window. They read: *On the wall to the left of the door leading out to Candy-Land, Our Revered Leader hangs ... but always slightly askew. That's my way of keeping him in perspective.*

I looked back at the picture. George Washington was gone, replaced by a photo of Franklin Roosevelt. F.D.R. had a grin on his face and his cigarette holder jutting upward at that angle his supporters think of as jaunty and his detractors as arrogant. The picture was hanging slightly askew.

"I don't need the laptop to do it," he said. He sounded a little embarrassed, as if I'd accused him of something. "I can do it just by concentrating—as you saw when the numbers disappeared from your blotter—but the laptop helps. Because I'm used to writing things down, I suppose. And then editing them. In a way, editing and rewriting are the most fascinating parts of the job, because that's where the final changes—usually small but often crucial—take place and the picture really comes into focus."

I looked back at Landry, and when I spoke, my voice was dead. "You made me up, didn't you?"

He nodded, looking strangely ashamed, as if what he had done was something dirty.

"When?" I uttered a strange, croaky little laugh. "Or is that the right question?"

"I don't know if it is or isn't," he said, "and I imagine any writer would tell you about the same. It didn't happen all at once—that much I'm sure of. It's been an ongoing process. You first showed up in *Scarlet Town*, but I wrote that back in 1977 and you've changed a lot since then."

1977, I thought. A Buck Rogers year for sure. I didn't want to believe this was happening, wanted to believe it was all a dream. Oddly enough, it was the smell of his cologne that kept me from being able to do that—that familiar smell I'd never smelled in my life. How could I have? It was Aramis, a brand as unfamiliar to me as Toshiba.

But he was going on.

"You've grown a lot more complex and interesting. You were pretty one-dimensional to start with." He cleared his throat and smiled down at his hands for a moment.

"What a pisser for me."

He winced a little at the anger in my voice, but made himself look up again, just the same. "Your last book was *How Like a Fallen Angel*. I started that one in 1990, but it took until 1993 to finish. I've had some problems in the interim. My life has been . . . interesting." He gave the word an ugly, bitter twist. "Writers don't do their best work during interesting times, Clyde. Take my word for it."

I glanced at the baggy way his hobo clothes hung on him and decided he might have a point there. "Maybe that's why you screwed up in such a big way on this one," I said. "That stuff about the lottery and the forty thousand dollars was pure guff—they pay off in pesos south of the border."

"I knew that," he said mildly. "I'm not saying I don't goof up from time to time—I may be a kind of God in this world, or *to* this world, but in my own I'm perfectly human—but when I *do* goof up, you and your fellow characters never know it, Clyde, because my mistakes and continuity lapses are part of your truth. No, Peoria was lying. I knew it, and I wanted *you* to know it."

"Why?"

He shrugged, again looking uneasy and a little ashamed. "To prepare you for my coming a little, I suppose. That's what all of it was for, starting with the Demmicks. I didn't want to scare you any more than I had to."

Any private eye worth his salt has a pretty good idea when the person in the client's chair is lying and when he's telling the truth; knowing when the client is telling the truth but purposely leaving gaps is a rarer talent, and

55

I doubt if even the geniuses among us can tap it all the time. Maybe I was only tapping it now because my brainwaves and Landry's were marching in lock-step, but I *was* tapping it. There was stuff he wasn't telling me. The question was whether or not I should call him on it.

What stopped me was a sudden, horrible intuition that came waltzing out of nowhere, like a ghost oozing out of the wall of a haunted house. It had to do with the Demmicks. The reason they'd been so quiet last night was because dead people don't engage in marital spats—it's one of those rules, like the one that says crap rolls downhill, that you can pretty much count on through thick and thin. From almost the first moment I'd met him, I'd sensed there was a violent temper under George's urbane top layer, and that there might be a sharp-clawed bitch lurking in the shadows behind Gloria Demmick's pretty face and daffy demeanor. They were just a little too Cole Porter to be true, if you see what I mean. And now I was somehow sure that George had finally snapped and killed his wife . . . probably their yappy Welsh Corgi, as well. Gloria might be sitting propped up in the bathroom corner between the shower and the toilet right now, her face black, her eyes bulging like old dull marbles, her tongue protruding between her blue lips. The dog was lying with its head in her lap and a wire coathanger twisted around

56

its neck, its shrill bark stilled forever. And George? Dead on the bed with Gloria's bottle of Veronals—now empty—standing beside him on the night-table. No more parties, no more jitterbugging at Al Arif, no more frothy upper-class murder cases in Palm Desert or Beverly Glen. They were cooling off now, drawing flies, growing pale under their fashionable poolside tans.

George and Gloria Demmick, who had died inside this man's machine. Who had died inside this man's *head*.

"You did one lousy job of not scaring me," I said, and immediately wondered if it would have been possible for him to do a good one. Ask yourself this: how do you get a person ready to meet God? I'll bet even Moses got a little hot under the robe when he saw that bush start to glow, and I'm nothing but a shamus who works for forty a day plus expenses.

"*How Like a Fallen Angel* was the Mavis Weld story. The name, Mavis Weld, is from a novel called *The Little Sister*. By Raymond Chandler." He looked at me with a kind of troubled uncertainty that had some small whiff of guilt in it. "It's an *hommage.*" He said the first syllable so it rhymed with Rome.

"Bully for you," I said, "but the guy's name rings no bells."

"Of course not. In your world—which is my version of

L.A., of course—Chandler never existed. Nevertheless, I've used all sorts of names from his books in mine. The Fulwider Building is where Chandler's detective, Philip Marlowe, had *his* office. Vernon Klein . . . Peoria Smith . . . and Clyde Umney, of course. That was the name of the lawyer in *Playback*."

"And you call those things *hommages?*"

"That's right."

"If you say so, but it sounds like a fancy word for plain old copying to me." But it made me feel funny, knowing that my name had been made up by a man I'd never heard of in a world I'd never dreamed of.

Landry had the good grace to flush, but his eyes didn't drop.

"All right; perhaps I *did* do a little pilfering. Certainly I adopted Chandler's style for my own, but I'm hardly the first; Ross Macdonald did the same thing in the fifties and sixties, Robert Parker did it in the seventies and eighties, and the critics decked them with laurel leaves for it. Besides, Chandler learned from Hammett and Hemingway, not to mention pulp-writers like—"

I held up my hand. "Let's skip the lit class and get down to the bottom line. This is crazy, but—" My eyes drifted to the picture of Roosevelt, from there they went to the eerily blank blotter, and from there they went back to the haggard face on the other side of the desk. "—but let's say I believe it. What are you doing here? What did you come for?"

Except I already knew. I detect for a living, but the answer to that one came from my heart, not my head.

"I came for *you.*"

"For me."

"Sorry, yes. I'm afraid you'll have to start thinking of your life in a new way, Clyde. As . . . well . . . a pair of shoes, let's say. You're stepping out and I'm stepping in. And once I've got the laces tied, I'm going to walk away."

Of course. Of course he was. And I suddenly knew what I had to do . . . the only thing I *could* do.

Get rid of him.

I let a big smile spread across my face. A tell-me-more smile. At the same time I coiled my legs under me, getting them ready to launch me across the desk at him. Only one of us could leave this office, that much was clear. I intended to be the one.

"Oh, *really?*" I said. "How fascinating. And what happens to me, Sammy? What happens to the shoeless private eye? What happens to Clyde—"

Umney, the last word was supposed to be my last name, the last word this interloping, invading thief would ever hear in his life. The minute it was out of my mouth I intended to leap. The trouble was, that telepathy business seemed to work both ways. I saw an expression of alarm dawn in his eyes, and then they slipped shut and his mouth tightened with concentration. He didn't bother with the Buck Rogers machine; I suppose he knew there was no time for it.

" 'His revelations hit me like some kind of debilitating drug,' " he said, speaking in the low but carrying tone of one who recites rather than simply speaking. " 'All the strength went out of my muscles, my legs felt like a couple of strands of *al dente* spaghetti, and all I could do was flop back in my chair and look at him.' "

I flopped back in my chair, my legs uncoiling beneath me, unable to do anything but look at him.

"Not very good," he said apologetically, "but rapid composition has never been a strong point of mine."

"You bastard," I rasped weakly. "You son of a bitch."

"Yes," he agreed. "I suppose I am."

"Why are you doing this? Why are you stealing my life?"

His eyes flickered with anger at that. "*Your* life? You know better than that, Clyde, even if you don't want to admit it. It isn't your life at all. I made you up, starting on one rainy day in January of 1977 and continuing right

60

up to the present time. I gave you your life, and it's mine to take away."

"Very noble," I sneered, "but if God came down here right now and started yanking *your* life apart like bad stitches in a scarf, you might find it a little easier to appreciate my point of view."

"All right," he said, "I suppose you've got a point. But why argue it? Arguing with one's self is like playing solitaire chess—a fair game results in a stalemate every time. Let's just say I'm doing it because I can."

I felt a little calmer, all of a sudden. I had been down this street before. When they got the drop on you, you had to get them talking and keep them talking. It had worked with Mavis Weld and it would work here. They said stuff like *Well, I suppose it won't hurt you to know now* or *What harm can it do?*

Mavis's version had been downright elegant: *I want you to know, Umney—I want you to take the truth to hell with you. You can pass it on to the devil over cake and coffee.* It really didn't matter what they said, but if they were talking, they weren't shooting.

Always keep em talking, that was the thing. Keep em talking and just hope the cavalry would show up from somewhere.

"The question is, why do you *want* to?" I asked. "It's

61

hardly the usual thing, is it? I mean, aren't you writer types usually content to cash the checks when they come, and go about your business?"

"You're trying to keep me talking, Clyde. Aren't you?"

That hit me like a sucker-punch to the gut, but playing it down to the last card was the only choice I had. I grinned and shrugged. "Maybe. Maybe not. Either way, I really do want to know." And there was no lie in that.

He looked unsure for a moment longer, bent over and touched the keys inside that strange plastic case (I felt cramps in my legs and gut and chest as he stroked them), then straightened up again.

"I suppose it won't hurt you to know now," he said finally. "After all, what harm can it do?"

"Not a bit."

"You're a clever boy, Clyde," he said, "and you're perfectly right—writers very rarely plunge all the way into the worlds they've created, and when they do I think they end up doing it strictly in their heads, while their bodies vegetate in some mental asylum. Most of us are content simply to be tourists in the country of our imaginations. Certainly that was the case with me. I'm not a fast writer—composition has always been torture for me, I think I told you that—but I managed five Clyde Umney books in ten years, each more successful than the last. In

1983 I left my job as regional manager for a big insurance company and started to write full-time. I had a wife I loved, a little boy that kicked the sun out of bed every morning and put it to bed every night—that's how it seemed to me, anyway—and I didn't think life could get any better."

He shifted in the overstuffed client's chair, moved his hand, and I saw the cigarette burn Ardis McGill had put in the overstuffed arm was also gone. He voiced a bitterly cold laugh.

"And I was right," he said. "It couldn't get any better, but it *could* get a whole hell of a lot worse. And did. About three months after I started *How Like a Fallen Angel*, Danny—our little boy—fell out of a swing in the park and bashed his head. Cold-conked himself, in your parlance."

A brief smile, every bit as cold and bitter as the laugh had been, crossed his face. It came and went at the speed of grief.

"He bled a lot—you've seen enough head-wounds in your time to know how they are—and it scared the crap out of Linda, but the doctors were good and it *did* turn out to be only a concussion; they got him stabilized and gave him a pint of blood to make up for what he'd lost. Maybe they didn't have to—and that haunts me—but

63

they did. The real problem wasn't with his head, you see; it was with that pint of blood. It was infected with AIDS."

"Come again?"

"It's something you can thank your God you don't know about," Landry said. "It doesn't exist in your time, Clyde. It won't show up until the mid-seventies. Like Aramis cologne."

"What does it do?"

"Eats away at your immune system until the whole thing collapses like the wonderful one-hoss shay. Then every bug circling around out there, from cancer to chicken pox, rushes in and has a party."

"Good Christ!"

His smile came and went like a cramp. "If you say so. AIDS is primarily a sexually transmitted disease, but every now and then it pops up in the blood supply. I suppose you could say my kid won big in a very unlucky version of *la lotería.*"

"I'm sorry," I said, and although I was scared to death of this thin man with the tired face, I meant it. Losing a kid to something like that . . . what could be worse? Probably something, yeah—there's always something—but you'd have to sit down and think about it, wouldn't you?

"Thanks," he said. "Thanks, Clyde. It went fast for

him, at least. He fell out of the swing in May. The first purple blotches—Kaposi's sarcoma—showed up in time for his birthday in September. He died on March 18, 1991. And maybe he didn't suffer as much as some of them do, but he suffered. Oh, yes, he suffered."

I didn't have the slightest idea what Kaposi's sarcoma was, either, and decided I didn't want to ask. I knew more than I wanted to already.

"You can maybe understand why it slowed me down a little on your book," he said. "Can't you, Clyde?"

I nodded.

"I pushed on, though. Mostly because I think make-believe is a great healer. Maybe I *have* to believe that. I tried to get on with my life, too, but things kept going wrong with it—it was as if *How Like a Fallen Angel* was some kind of weird bad-luck charm that had turned me into Job. My wife went into a deep depression following Danny's death, and I was so concerned with her that I hardly noticed the red patches that had started breaking out on my legs and stomach and chest. And the itching. I knew it wasn't AIDS, and at first that was all I was concerned with. But as time went on and things got worse . . . have you ever had shingles, Clyde?"

Then he laughed and clapped the heel of his hand to

65

his forehead in a what-a-dunce-I-am gesture before I could shake my head.

"Of course you haven't—you've never had more than a hangover. Shingles, my shamus friend, is a funny name for a terrible, chronic ailment. There's some pretty good medicine available to help alleviate the symptoms in my version of Los Angeles, but it wasn't helping me much; by the end of 1991 I was in agony. Part of it was general depression over what had happened to Danny, of course, but most of it was the agony and the itching. That would make an interesting book title about a tortured writer, don't you think? *The Agony and the Itching, or, Thomas Hardy Faces Puberty.*" He voiced a harsh, distracted little laugh.

"Whatever you say, Sam."

"I say it was a season in hell. Of course it's easy to make light of it now, but by Thanksgiving of that year it was no joke—I was getting three hours of sleep a night, tops, and I had days when it felt like my skin was trying to crawl right off my body and run away like The Gingerbread Man. And I suppose that's why I didn't see how bad it was getting with Linda."

I didn't know, *couldn't* know . . . but I did. "She killed herself."

He nodded. "In March of 1992, on the anniversary of Daniel's death. Over two years ago now."

A single tear tracked down his wrinkled, prematurely aged cheek, and I had an idea that he had gotten old in one hell of a hurry. It was sort of awful, realizing I had been made by such a bush-league version of God, but it also explained a lot. My shortcomings, mainly.

"That's enough," he said in a voice which was blurred with anger as well as tears. "Get to the point, you'd say. In my time we say cut to the chase, but it comes to the same. I finished the book. On the day I discovered Linda dead in bed—the way the police are going to find Gloria Demmick later today, Clyde—I had finished one hundred and ninety pages of manuscript. I was up to the part where you fish Mavis's brother out of Lake Tahoe. I came home from the funeral three days later, fired up the word-processor, and got started right in on page one-ninety-one. Does that shock you?"

"No," I said. I thought about asking him what a word-processor might be, then decided I didn't have to. The thing in his lap was a word-processor, of course. Had to be.

"You're in a decided minority," Landry said. "It shocked what few friends I had left, shocked them plenty. Linda's relatives thought I had all the emotion of a warthog. I didn't have the energy to explain that I was trying to save myself. Frog them, as Peoria would say. I grabbed my book the way a drowning man would grab a life-ring. I grabbed *you*, Clyde. My case of the shingles was still bad, and that slowed me down—to some extent it kept me *out*, or I might have gotten here sooner—but it didn't stop me. I started getting a little better—physically, at least—right around the time I finished the book. But when I *had* finished, I fell into what I suppose must have been my own state of depression. I went through the edited script in a kind of daze. I felt such a feeling of regret ... of *loss* ... " He looked directly at me and said, "Does any of this make any sense to you?"

"It makes sense," I said. And it did. In a crazy sort of way.

"There were lots of pills left in the house," he said. "Linda and I were like the Demmicks in a lot of ways, Clyde—we really did believe in living better chemically, and a couple of times I came very close to taking a couple of double handfuls. The way the thought always came to me wasn't in terms of suicide, but in terms of wanting to catch up to Linda and Danny. To catch up while there was still time."

I nodded. It was what I'd thought about Ardis McGill when, three days after we'd said toodle-oo to each other in Blondie's, I'd found her in that stuffy attic room with a small blue hole in the center of her forehead. Except it had been Sam Landry who had really killed her, and who had accomplished the deed with a kind of flexible bullet to the brain. Of course it had been. In my world Sam Landry, this tired-looking man in the hobo's pants, was responsible for *everything*. The idea should have seemed crazy, and it did . . . but it was getting saner all the time.

I found I had just energy enough to swivel my chair and look out my window. What I saw somehow did not surprise me in the least: Sunset Boulevard and all that surrounded it had frozen solid. Cars, buses, pedestrians, all stopped dead in their tracks. It was a Kodak snapshot world out there, and why not? Its creator could not be bothered with animating much of it, at least for the time being; he was still caught in the whirlpool of his own pain and grief. Hell, I was lucky to still be breathing myself.

"So what happened?" I asked. "How did you get here, Sam? Can I call you that? Do you mind?"

"No, I don't mind. I can't give you a very good answer, though, because I don't exactly know. All I know for sure is that every time I thought of the pills, I thought of you. What I thought specifically was, 'Clyde Umney would never do this, and he'd sneer at anyone who did. He'd call it the coward's way out.' "

I considered that, found it fair enough, and nodded. For someone staring some horrible ailment in the face—Vernon's cancer, or the misbegotten nightmare that had killed this man's son—I might make an exception, but take the pipe just because you were depressed? That was for pansies.

"Then I thought, 'But that's Clyde Umney, and Clyde is make-believe . . . just a figment of your imagination.' That idea wouldn't live, though. It's the dumbbells of the world—politicians and lawyers, for the most part—who sneer at imagination, and think a thing isn't real unless they can smoke it or stroke it or feel it or fuck it. They think that way because they have no imagination themselves, and they have no idea of its power. I knew better. Hell, I ought to—my imagination has been buying my food and paying the mortgage for the last ten years or so.

"At the same time, I knew I couldn't go on living in what I used to think of as 'the real world,' by which I suppose we all mean 'the only world.' That's when I started to realize there was only one place left where I could go and feel welcome, and only one person I could be when I got there. The place was here—Los Angeles, in 1930-something. And the person was you."

I heard that faint whirring sound coming from inside his gadget again, but I didn't turn around.

Partly because I was afraid to.

And partly because I no longer knew if I could.

VI. Umney's Last Case.

On the street seven stories below, a man was frozen with his head half-turned to look at the woman on the corner, who was climbing up the step of the eight-fifty bus headed downtown. She had exposed a momentary length of beautiful leg, and this was what the man was looking at. A little farther down the street a boy was holding out his battered old baseball glove to catch the ball frozen in mid-air just above his head. And, floating six feet above the street like a ghost called up by a third-rate swami at a carnival séance, was one of the newspapers from Peoria Smith's overturned table. Incredibly, I could see the two photographs on it from up here: Hitler above the fold, the recently deceased Cuban bandleader below it.

Landry's voice seemed to come from a long way off.

"At first I thought that meant I'd be spending the rest of my life in some nut-ward, thinking I was you, but that was all right, because it would only be my *physical* self locked up in the funny-farm, do you see? And then, gradually, I began to realize that it could be a lot more than

72

that . . . that maybe there might be a way I could actually
. . . well . . . slip all the way in. And do you know what
the key was?"

"Yes," I said, not looking around. That whir came
again as something in his gadget revolved, and suddenly
the newspaper frozen in mid-air flapped off down the frozen Boulevard. A moment or two later an old DeSoto
rolled jerkily through the intersection of Sunset and
Fernando. It struck the boy wearing the baseball glove,
and both he and the DeSoto sedan disappeared. Not the
ball, though. It fell into the street, rolled half-way to the
gutter, then froze solid again.

"You do?" He sounded surprised.

"Yeah. Peoria was the key."

"That's right." He laughed, then cleared his throat—
nervous sounds, both of them. "I keep forgetting that
you're me."

It was a luxury I didn't have.

"I was fooling around with a new book, and not getting
anywhere. I'd tried Chapter One six different ways to
Sunday before realizing a really interesting thing: Peoria
Smith didn't like you."

That made me swing around in a hurry. "The hell you
say!"

"I didn't think you'd believe it, but it's the truth, and

73

I'd somehow known it all along. I don't want to convene the lit class again, Clyde, but I'll tell you one thing about my trade—writing stories in the first person is a funny, tricky business. It's as if everything the writer knows comes from his main character, like a series of letters or dispatches from some far-off battle zone. It's very rare for the writer to have a secret, but in this case I did. It was as if your little part of Sunset Boulevard were the Garden of Eden—"

"I never heard it called *that* before," I remarked.

"—and there was a snake in it, one I saw and you didn't. A snake named Peoria Smith."

Outside, the frozen world that he'd called my Garden of Eden continued to darken, although the sky was cloudless. The Red Door, a nightclub reputedly owned by Lucky Luciano, disappeared. For a moment there was just a hole where it had been, and then a new building filled it—a restaurant called Petit Déjeuner with a window full of ferns. I glanced up the street and saw that other changes were going on—new buildings were replacing old ones with silent, spooky speed. They meant I was running out of time; I knew this. Unfortunately, I knew something else, as well—there was probably not going to be any nick in this bundle of time. When God walks into your office and tells you He's decided he likes your life better than His own, what the hell are your options?

"I junked all the various drafts of the novel I'd started two months after my wife's death," Landry said. "It was easy—poor crippled things that they were. And then I started a new one. I called it . . . can you guess, Clyde?"

"Sure," I said, and swung around. It took all my strength, but what I suppose this geek would call my "motivation" was good. Sunset Strip isn't exactly the Champs Elysées or Hyde Park, but it's my world. I didn't want to watch him tear it apart and rebuild it the way *he* wanted it. "I suppose you called it *Umney's Last Case.*"

He looked faintly surprised. "You suppose right."

I waved my hand. It was an effort, but I managed. "I didn't win the Shamus of the Year Award in 1934 and '35 for nothing, you know."

He smiled at that. "Yes. I always *did* like that line."

Suddenly I hated him—hated him like poison. If I could have summoned the strength to lunge across the desk and choke the life out of him, I would have done it. He saw it, too. The smile faded.

"Forget it, Clyde—you wouldn't have a chance."

"Why don't you get out of here?" I grated at him. "Just get out and let a working stiff alone?"

"Because I can't. I couldn't even if I wanted to . . . and

I don't." He looked at me with an odd mixture of anger and pleading. "Try to look at it from my point of view, Clyde—"

"Do I have any choice? Have I ever?"

He ignored that. "Here's a world where I'll never get any older, a year where all the clocks are stopped at just about eighteen months before World War II, where the newspapers always cost three cents, where I can eat all the eggs and red meat I want and never have to worry about my cholesterol level."

"I don't have the slightest idea what you're talking about."

He leaned forward earnestly. "No, you don't! And that's exactly the point, Clyde! This is a world where I can *really* do the job I dreamed about doing when I was a little boy—I can be a private eye. I can go racketing around in a fast car at two in the morning, shoot it out with hoodlums—knowing they may die but I won't—and wake up eight hours later next to a beautiful *chanteuse* with the birds twittering in the trees and the sun shining in my bedroom window. That clear, beautiful California sun."

"My bedroom window faces west," I said.

"Not anymore," he replied calmly, and I felt my hands curl into strengthless fists on the arms of my chair. "Do you see how wonderful it is? How perfect? In this world, people don't go half-mad with itching caused by a stupid, undignified disease called shingles. In this world, people don't go gray, let alone bald."

He looked at me levelly, and in his gaze I saw no hope for me. No hope at all.

"In this world, beloved sons never die of AIDS and beloved wives never take overdoses of sleeping pills. Besides, you were *always* the outsider here, not me, no matter how it might have felt to you. This is *my* world, born in my imagination and maintained by my effort and ambition. I loaned it to you for awhile, that's all . . . and now I'm taking it back."

"Finish telling me how you got in, will you do that much? I really want to hear."

"It was easy. I tore it apart, starting with the Demmicks, who were never much more than a lousy imitation of Nick and Nora Charles, and rebuilt it in my own image. I took away all the beloved supporting characters, and now I'm removing all the old landmarks. I'm pulling the rug out from under you a strand at a time, in other words, and I'm not proud of it, but I *am* proud of the sustained effort of will it's taken to pull it off."

"What's happened to you back in your own world?" I was still keeping him talking, but now it was nothing but habit, like an old milk-horse finding his way back to the barn on a snowy morning.

He shrugged. "Dead, maybe. Or maybe I really have left a physical self—a husk—sitting catatonic in some mental institution. I don't think either of those things is really the case, though—all of this feels too real. No, I think I made it all the way, Clyde. I think that back home they're looking for a missing writer . . . with no idea that he's disappeared into the storage banks of his own word-processor. And the truth is I really don't care."

"And me? What happens to me?"

"Clyde," he said, "I don't care about that, either."

He bent over his gadget again.

"Don't!" I said sharply.

He looked up.

"I . . ." I heard the quiver in my voice, tried to control it, and found I couldn't. "Mister, I'm afraid. Please leave me alone. I know it's not really my world out there anymore—hell, in here, either—but it's the only world I'll ever come close to knowing. Let me have what's left of it. Please."

"Too late, Clyde." Again I heard that merciless regret in his voice. "Close your eyes. I'll make it as fast as I can."

I tried to jump him—I tried as hard as I could. I didn't

move so much as an iota. And as far as closing my eyes went, I discovered I didn't need to. All the light had gone out of the day, and the office was as dark as midnight in a coalsack.

I sensed rather than saw him lean over the desk toward me. I tried to draw back and discovered I couldn't even do that. Something dry and rustly touched my hand and I screamed.

"Take it easy, Clyde." His voice, coming out of the darkness. Coming not just from in front of me but from everywhere. *Of course,* I thought. *After all, I'm a figment of his imagination.* "It's only a check."

"A . . . check?"

"Yes. For five thousand dollars. You've sold me the business. The painters will scratch your name off the door and paint mine on before they leave tonight." He sounded dreamy. "Samuel D. Landry, Private Detective. It's got a great ring, doesn't it?"

I tried to beg and found I couldn't. Now even my voice had failed me.

"Get ready," he said. "I don't know exactly what's coming, Clyde, but it's coming now. I don't think it'll hurt." *But I don't really care if it does*—that was the part he didn't say.

That faint whirring sound came out of the blackness. I

felt my chair melt away beneath me, and suddenly I was falling. Landry's voice fell with me, reciting along with the clicks and taps of his fabulous futuristic steno machine, reciting the last two sentences of a novel called *Umney's Last Case.*

" 'So I left town, and as to where I finished up . . . well, mister, I think that's my business. Don't you?' "

There was a brilliant green light below me. I was falling toward it. Soon it would consume me, and the only feeling I had was one of relief.

" 'THE END,' " Landry's voice boomed, and then I fell into the green light, it was shining through me, *in* me, and Clyde Umney was no more.

So long, shamus.

VII. The Other Side of the Light.

All that was six months ago.

I came to on the floor of a gloomy room with a humming in my ears, pushed myself to my knees, shook my head to clear it, and looked up into the bright green glare I'd fallen through, like Alice through the looking glass. I saw a Buck Rogers machine that was the big brother of the one Landry had brought into my office. Green letters shone on it and I pushed myself to my feet so I could read them, absently running my fingernails up and down over my lower arms as I did so:

So I left town, and as to where I finished up . . . well, mister, I think that's my business. Don't you?

And below that, capitalized and centered, two more words:

THE END.

I read it again, now running my fingers over my stomach. I was doing it because there was something wrong with my skin, something that wasn't exactly painful but *was* certainly bothersome. As soon as it rose to the fore in my mind, I realized that weird sensation was going on everywhere—the nape of my neck, the backs of my thighs, in my crotch.

Shingles, I thought suddenly. *I've got Landry's shingles. What I'm feeling is itching, and the reason I didn't recognize it right away is because—*

"Because I've never *had* an itch before," I said, and then the rest of it clicked into place. The click was so sudden and so hard that I actually swayed on my feet. I walked slowly across to a mirror on the wall, trying not to scratch my weirdly crawling skin, knowing I was going to see an aged version of my face, a face cut with lines like old dry washes and topped with a shock of lackluster white hair.

Now I knew what happened when writers somehow took over the lives of the characters they had created. It wasn't exactly theft after all.

More of a swap.

I stood staring into Landry's face—*my* face, only aged fifteen hard years—and felt my skin tingling and buzzing. Hadn't he said his shingles had been getting better? If this was better, how had he endured worse without going completely insane?

I was in Landry's house, of course—my house, now—and in the bathroom off the study, I found the medication he took for his shingles. I took my first dose less than an hour after I came to on the floor below his desk and the humming machine on it, and it was as if I had swallowed his life instead of medicine.

As if I'd swallowed his whole life.

These days the shingles are a thing of the past, I'm happy to report. Maybe it just ran its course, but I like to think that the old Clyde Umney spirit had something to do with it—Clyde was never sick a day in his life, you know, and although I seem to always have the sniffles in this run-down Sam Landry body, I'll be damned if I'll give in to them . . . and since when did it hurt to turn on a little of that positive thinking? I think the correct answer to that one is "since never."

There have been some pretty bad days, though, the first one coming less than twenty-four hours after I showed up in the unbelievable year of 1994. I was looking through Landry's fridge for something to eat (I'd pigged out on his Black Horse Ale the night before and felt it couldn't hurt my hangover to eat something) when a sudden pain knifed into my guts. I thought I was dying. It got worse, and I *knew* I was dying. I fell to the kitchen floor, trying not to scream. A moment or two later, something happened, and the pain eased.

Most of my life I've been using the phrase "I don't give a shit." All that has changed, starting that morning. I cleaned myself up, then climbed the stairs, knowing what I'd find in the bedroom: wet sheets in Landry's bed.

My first week in Landry's world was spent mostly in toilet-training myself. In my world, of course, nobody ever went to the bathroom. Or to the dentist, for that matter, and my first trip to the one listed in Landry's Rolodex is something I don't even want to think about, let alone discuss.

But there's been an occasional rose in this nest of brambles. For one thing, there's been no need to go job-hunting in Landry's confusing, jet-propelled world; his books apparently continue to sell very well, and I have no problem cashing the checks that come in the mail. My signature and his are, of course, identical. As for any moral compunctions I might have about doing that, don't make me laugh. Those checks are for stories about *me*. Landry only wrote them; I lived them. Hell, I deserved fifty thou and a rabies shot just for getting within scratching distance of Mavis Weld's claws.

I expected to have problems with Landry's so-called friends, but I suppose a heavy-duty shamus like me should have known better—would a guy with any real friends want to disappear into a world he'd created on the soundstage of his own imagination? Not likely. Landry's friends were his son and his wife, and they were dead. There are acquaintances and neighbors, but they seem to accept me as him. The woman across the street throws me puzzled glances from time to time, and her little girl cries when I come near even though I used to baby-sit for them every now and then (the woman *says* I did, anyway, and why would she lie?), but that's no big deal.

I have even spoken to Landry's agent, a guy from New York named Verrill. He wants to know when I'm going to start a new book.

Soon, I tell him. Soon.

Mostly I stay in. I have no urge to explore the world Landry pushed me into when he pushed me out of my own; I see more than I want to on my once-weekly trip to the bank and the grocery store, and I threw a bookend through his awful television machine less than two hours after I figured out how to use it. It doesn't surprise me that Landry wanted to leave this groaning world with its freight of disease and senseless violence—a world where naked women dance in nightclub windows, and sex with them can kill you.

No, I spend my time inside, mostly. I have re-read each

of his novels, and each one is like leafing through the pages of a well-loved scrapbook. And I've taught myself to use his word-processing machine, of course. It's not like the television machine; the screen is similar, but on the word-processor, you can make whatever pictures *you* want to see, because they all come from inside your own head.

I like that.

I've been getting ready, you see—trying sentences and discarding them the way you try pieces in a jigsaw puzzle. And this morning I wrote a few that seem right . . . or *almost* right. Want to hear? Okay, here goes:

When I looked toward the door, I saw a very chastened, very downcast Peoria Smith standing there. "I guess I treated you pretty bad the last time I saw you, Mr. Umney," he said. "I came to say I'm sorry." It had been over six months, but he looked the same as ever. And I do mean the same.

"You're still wearing your cheaters," I said.

"Yeah. We tried the operation, but it didn't work." He sighed, then grinned and shrugged. In that moment he looked like the Peoria I'd always known. "What the hey, Mr. Umney—bein blind ain't so bad."

It isn't perfect; sure, I know that. I started out as a detective, not a writer. But I believe you can do just about anything, if you want to bad enough, and when you get

86

right down to where the cheese binds, this is a kind of keyhole-peeping, too. The size and shape of the word-processor keyhole are a little different, but it's still looking into other people's lives and then reporting back to the client on what you saw.

I'm teaching myself for one very simple reason: I don't want to be here. You can call it L.A. in 1994 if you want to; I call it hell. It's awful frozen dinners you cook in a box called a "microwave," it's sneakers that look like Frankenstein shoes, it's music that comes out of the radio sounding like crows being steamed alive in a pressure-cooker, it's—

Well, it's *everything*.

I want my life back, I want things the way they were, and I think I know how to make that happen.

You're one sad, thieving bastard, Sam—may I still call you that?—and I feel sorry for you . . . but sorry only stretches so far, because the operant word here is *thieving*. My original opinion on the subject hasn't changed at all, you see—I still don't believe that the ability to create conveys the right to steal.

What are you doing right this minute, you thief? Eating dinner at that Petit Déjeuner restaurant you made up? Sleeping beside some gorgeous honey with perfect no-sag breasts and murder up the sleeve of her negligee? Driving down to Malibu with carefree abandon? Or just kicking back in the old office chair, enjoying your painless, odorless, shitless life? What are you doing?

I've been teaching myself to write, that's what *I've* been doing, and now that I've found my way in, I think I'll get better in a hurry. Already I can almost see you.

Tomorrow morning, Clyde and Peoria are going to go down to Blondie's, which has re-opened for business. This time Peoria's going to take Clyde up on that breakfast offer. That will be step two.

Yes, I can almost see you, Sam, and pretty soon I will. But I don't think you'll see me. Not until I step out from behind my office door and wrap my hands around your throat.

This time nobody goes home.

FOR THE BEST IN PAPERBACKS, LOOK FOR THE

In every corner of the world, on every subject under the sun, Penguin represents quality and variety—the very best in publishing today.

For complete information about books available from Penguin—including Puffins, Penguin Classics, and Arkana—and how to order them, write to us at the appropriate address below. Please note that for copyright reasons the selection of books varies from country to country.

In the United States: Please write to *Consumer Sales, Penguin USA, P.O. Box 999, Dept. 17109, Bergenfield, New Jersey 07621-0120.* VISA and MasterCard holders call 1-800-253-6476 to order all Penguin titles.

In Canada: Please write to *Penguin Books Canada Ltd, 10 Alcorn Avenue, Suite 300, Toronto, Ontario M4V 3B2.*

In the United Kingdom: Please write to *Dept. JC, Penguin Books Ltd, FREEPOST, West Drayton, Middlesex UB7 0BR.*